Blackfire

Adapted by Tracey West
Based on the episode *Sisters* written by Amy Wolfram
Illustrated by Kevin MacKenzie

Scholastic Inc.
New York   Toronto   London   Auckland   Sydney
Mexico City   New Delhi   Hong Kong   Buenos Aires

ISBN: 0-439-63618-3

Published by Scholastic Inc.
SCHOLASTIC and associated logos are trademarks and/or registered trademarks of Scholastic Inc.

12 11 10 9 8 7 6 5 4 3   5 6 7 8 9/0

Designed by Carisa Swenson
Printed in the U.S.A.
First printing, August 2004

Chapter One

Fire in the Sky

Being a Teen Titan is a lot of hard work. Keeping the world safe from evildoers means hours of training and fighting — not to mention keeping your costume wrinkle-free.

But even super heroes get to chill out once in a while. That's what the Teen Titans were doing one starry summer night. They had gone to the carnival. Beast Boy, Cyborg, and Raven decided to try their luck at the game booths. Robin and Starfire opted for the Ferris wheel. They were just in time, too. A fireworks display lit up the sky over the nearby river, and Robin and Starfire had a perfect view.

BOOM! A shower of green and gold shimmered

against the deep blue sky. *BOOM!* Next came bursts of purple, red, and blue.

Starfire rested her chin in her hands, gazing at the fireworks. With her long, red hair, green eyes, and purple costume, she looked even more colorful than the fiery display in the sky.

"On my home planet, such explosions would mean the Gordanians were attacking," Starfire remarked, a touch of worry in her voice. "You are certain Earth is not under attack?"

"Positive," Robin said. He held out a paper cone filled with a cloud of pink spun sugar. "Cotton candy?"

Starfire frowned. "The last time I ate a ball of cotton it was white and did not taste very —"

"This is different," Robin assured her. He pulled off a piece and popped it in his mouth.

Starfire did the same. "Mmm," she said, smiling. Then she gave a little gasp. "It vanished!"

"Yeah, it'll do that," Robin said, smiling back. Starfire had only been on Earth a short time, and most things were new to her — like the sensation of cotton candy melting in your mouth.

Starfire sighed happily. "When I first came to this planet, I did not think I would ever fit in. Earth was full of strange things, but now I see that —"

Robin interrupted her again. "Here comes the finale! Yes!" he cried, as the sound of exploding fireworks filled the air once again.

BOOM! BOOM! BOOM! Streaks of pink, gold, and silver light exploded in the night sky and then tumbled down into the water.

"Whoo-hoo! Amazing!" Robin cried, pumping his fists in the air.

Starfire looked at Robin. "Earth is full of amazing things," she said softly.

"Best planet I've ever been to," Robin agreed.

Suddenly, Starfire let out a piercing scream. Robin watched in shock as a metal capsule with four pink tentacles swooped past Starfire. The tentacles grabbed her — and then the pod flew up and away!

"Starfire!" Robin yelled.

Chapter Two

What Was That Thing?

Back on the ground, Cyborg tossed a red ring over the neck of a glass bottle. "Boo-yah!" cried the half-teen, half-robot.

The worker in the booth handed the prize to Beast Boy, who was half the size of Cyborg, with green skin and hair. His eyes lit up as he accepted the giant stuffed chicken.

"Sweet!" he cried. He handed it over to Raven, a pale girl wearing a blue cape and hood. "Told you we'd win you a prize."

Raven's expression did not change. "A giant chicken. I must be the luckiest girl in the world," she said in a flat voice that meant she felt exactly the opposite.

Just then, Robin ran up, his yellow cape flapping behind him. "Titans! Trouble!"

"Where's Starfire?" Cyborg asked.

"That's the trouble," Robin replied. Without another word, he ran off toward the pier. Raven tossed the chicken aside and she, Cyborg, and Beast Boy chased after Robin.

Overhead, the pod flew across the river with Starfire still in its clutches.

"Wherever you are taking me, I do not wish to go," Starfire told it. A green light shot from her eyes, zapping the pink tentacles. The tentacles let

go of her, and she flew away as quickly as she could. But the pod followed right behind her.

A tentacle whipped out and tried to grab Starfire again. She dodged it, then turned around and flew backward, facing the pod. She blasted it with a green beam of light from her left hand, then one from her right.

"No more chasing now, please!" she cried.

As the Teen Titans watched, Starfire flew down toward the pier. She whizzed past them with the pod in hot pursuit.

"Who's her new best friend?" Beast Boy asked.

Robin slammed his fist into his hand. "I don't know, but I can't wait to meet him."

Starfire circled around the Ferris wheel and then flew back toward her friends. She hovered above them and faced the pod, her green eyes blazing.

The Teen Titans jumped in to help. Beast Boy transformed into an alligator and charged at the pod, his powerful jaws snapping — but the pod dodged him. Raven used her powers of levitation to raise a heavy hot-dog cart off the ground and send it hurtling toward the pod. But the hot-dog cart smashed to pieces when it made contact.

Next, Cyborg grabbed the pod's pink tentacles. "Don't know what you did to make this thing mad, Star," Cyborg said, struggling to keep the pod in his grasp, "but it couldn't hurt to apologize!"

"I am sorry?" Starfire told the pod. But it didn't seem to make a difference. The pod broke free of

Cyborg's hold.

But Robin didn't let it get far. He whacked it with his fighting staff. The blow sent the pod hurtling over the pier and splashing into the river. It didn't emerge.

Beast Boy looked over the railing. "So, did we just win?"

Before anyone could answer, the pod burst through the wood planks of the pier! Acting quickly, Robin jumped up and rode the pod like a cowboy riding a bucking bronco.

"Don't see an off switch," Robin said. "Guess I'll have to make one!"

In one swift motion, Robin reached down into the nose of the pod and pulled out a bunch of wires. Then he quickly jumped off, landing safely on the pier.

He got away just in time. The pod spiraled up into the sky, and then exploded, adding a huge shower of orange and yellow sparks to the fireworks display.

Robin walked over to Starfire, who stood on the pier, watching the sky.

"Whatever that thing was, it can't hurt you anymore," Robin said.

Starfire frowned. "But why did it wish to hurt me at all?"

Chapter Three

Sisters

The Teen Titans headed back to their head-quarters — a tall, *T*-shaped building over-looking the river. The elevator door opened on to the central room, and Starfire stepped out first.

"Come, friends," she said, holding out her arms. "I shall thank you all by reciting the Poem of Gratitude — all six thousand verses!"

The other Titans groaned softly. But before they could protest, a strange voice rang through the room.

"I see you haven't changed a bit."

A teenage girl with long, black hair and slanted, violet eyes was leaning against the back of the

couch. She wore black boots, silver tights, black shorts, and a black-and-silver top.

"When we were little, I was always rescuing Starfire," the girl continued.

Starfire ran over and threw her arms around the girl. "Ah! Sister!" she cried happily.

"Brought you a present," said Starfire's sister. She held out a glittering green gem dangling from a chain.

Starfire's eyes grew wide. "A Centauri moon diamond? Where did you get it?"

Starfire's sister hung the chain around Starfire's neck. "On the Centauri moons, of course. Oh, look, it matches your eyes!"

Starfire grabbed her sister by the arm and dragged her across the room to the other Teen Titans. "You must meet my friends," she said excitedly. "I wish to introduce you to my big sister —"

"Blackfire," finished the girl. "And since Star told me all about the Titans in her transmissions, let me guess."

Blackfire walked in front of Cyborg. "Cyborg, right?"

Cyborg held out his large, metal hand. "Pleased to meet you, little lady."

Blackfire grinned and grabbed his hand. When the handshake was finished, Cyborg's metal hand was crushed. He was impressed.

"Little lady, big handshake. Well, all right!"

Blackfire moved to Raven and pointed to the small, diamond-shaped gem in the middle of her forehead.

"Raven. I like that gemstone on your ashma chakra," she remarked.

Raven raised an eyebrow. "You know about chakras?" She rarely met anyone who could talk about the seven major energy vortexes on the human body.

"I got way into meditation on Altara Prime," Blackfire explained. Then she moved over to Beast Boy.

"Beast Boy, what's up?"

Beast Boy pointed up with his finger. "Nothing but the ceiling, baby!"

Blackfire laughed. "Good one!"

Beast Boy turned to Raven. "See? She thinks I'm funny," he whispered.

"Statistically, I suppose somebody has to," Raven replied.

Meanwhile, Blackfire had moved to Robin. She jumped behind him and grabbed his cape.

"And you must be Robin," she said. "I am loving this cape! It is positively luscious."

"Thanks," Robin said. "It's a high-density plasmarized titanium. Ten times stronger than steel."

"Fascinating," Blackfire said, moving closer. "And this mask makes you look *very* mysterious."

Starfire jumped between them. "So, beloved sister, what brings you to Earth?"

"I was in the quadrant. Thought I'd see if earthlings like to party," she said casually. She jumped over the arm of the couch and lounged on the cushions. "Besides, I needed a rest. I nearly got

sucked into a black hole on the way here."

Immediately, Robin, Cyborg, and Beast Boy surrounded her.

"Black hole?" Robin asked.

"Cool!" Beast Boy cried.

"No way!" added Cyborg. All three boys had
their eyes glued to Blackfire.

Blackfire grinned, loving the attention. "So I'm
cruising through the Draconus nebula and —"

"Sister!" Starfire said, shocked. "That nebula is *full* of black holes. You know travel there is forbidden."

"Most fun things in life are," Blackfire said. "Now, be a sweetie and bring me one of those sodas I've heard so much about."

Starfire scowled as she headed to the refrigerator. She had been so happy to see Blackfire, but she had almost forgotten what her big sister was like. Always doing dangerous stunts, ordering Starfire around — and stealing all the attention wherever she went.

"I see you have not changed, yourself," Starfire muttered under her breath. Then she slammed the refrigerator door shut .

Chapter Four

Find the Girl!

While Blackfire entertained the Teen Titans with stories of her adventures, three more pods sailed across the night sky. They looked just like the pod that had been chasing Starfire. Pink tentacles trailed beneath each silver pod.

One by one, the pods flew into a round entry port on the bottom of a large, black spaceship. Each pod shot down a chute and emerged in a clear glass tube. When the pod returned, a green light came on at the bottom of the tube.

Two aliens watched as the pods came back. The tall aliens looked like they were encased in red armor. Thick, black spikes protruded from their

forearms. Their lower arms looked like huge lobster claws. Each alien's square, severe-looking head had a speaker where the mouth should be.

The third pod came to rest in its tube. But a fourth tube stood empty. The light at the bottom of the tube blinked red.

"Our target was not located," one of the aliens said in a deep voice. "The pods have failed."

"Have they?" asked the other alien. A metal rod emerged from his claw and touched a nearby computer screen. A picture of Earth appeared.

"The one that probed Earth has not returned. That is where we will find the girl."

The two aliens stared at the screen and nodded. They would travel to Earth and find the girl.

They would not go home empty-handed.

Chapter Five

Queen of the Galaxy

The next morning, Starfire tried to muster a positive attitude. Growing up in Blackfire's shadow had not been easy. But Blackfire was her sister, after all, and they had not seen each other in a long time. Perhaps Starfire could show Blackfire around town.

Finding Blackfire wasn't easy. Starfire searched all over Teen Titans' headquarters.

"Sister? Sister? I seek your companionship," Starfire called out.

She found Cyborg and Beast Boy sitting on the couch, playing a video game. Both boys were frantically pushing buttons on their control pads, their eyes fixed on the television screen.

23

Cyborg taunted Beast Boy. "You want to pass me. But you can't pass me! You can't pass me!" Then he frowned. "Huh? You passed me!"

"Tighten the turn, jet, and nitro!" Beast Boy crowed, standing up to do a victory dance. Then he sat back down and continued pressing buttons.

"Tell me, has either of you seen Blackfire?" Starfire asked them.

"Blazing B? She was here just a second ago," Beast Boy replied.

"It looks like fun," Starfire asked. "May I join your game?" If she couldn't find Blackfire, she could at least have fun with her friends.

But Cyborg shook his head. "Winner plays Blackfire," he said.

"She rocks at this game!" Beast Boy added.

"I see," Starfire said. Her positive attitude was rapidly disappearing.

Starfire knocked on Raven's door next. The door slid partway open, revealing half of Raven's

always-serious face.

"Is my sister in there?" Starfire asked.

"No," Raven said simply.

"Might you wish to hang out with me?" Starfire asked. "We could visit your favorite depressing café."

"Already did," Raven said. "It was open mike, and Blackfire wanted to share. Your sister's poetry is surprisingly dark."

Raven shut the door, and Starfire sighed. Why was it so easy for Blackfire to fit in? She hadn't even been here a day, and she had already figured out how to do all kinds of Earth things. Starfire still felt like she didn't belong.

Starfire headed to the training room next. She knew she would probably find Robin there. He was her closest friend among the Teen Titans. Surely Robin would have some time to hang out with her.

As she walked down the hallway, she saw a shadow on the wall. It looked like Robin and Blackfire — hugging! The she heard Blackfire's voice.

"That's perfect, Robin," she said. "Hold it just like that and — hi-yah!"

Starfire gasped and ran into the training room — just in time to see Blackfire throw Robin across the room. Robin jumped to his feet.

"Learned that move from a Venzo master on Taras three," Blackfire said proudly.

Starfire cleared her throat. "Hello Robin and . . . my sister. Am I interrupting?"

"Not at all," Robin said cheerfully. "Blackfire was just showing me some alien martial arts. How come you never taught me these cool moves?"

"Probably because she doesn't know them," Blackfire said. "I always was the better fighter."

Starfire stomped out of the room. Better fighter? Maybe when they were growing up. But Starfire had worked hard on her fighting skills. After all, who was the Teen Titan? Not her sister, that was for sure.

Starfire tried to calm down and bring back her positive attitude. The other Titans liked Blackfire because she was fun. Well, she could be fun, too.

A few hours later, Starfire entered the main room with her arms full of DVDs and buckets of snacks. Robin, Beast Boy, Cyborg, and Raven sat on the circular red couch in the middle of the room. Raven had her face buried in a book.

"Friends, I invite you to join me in the togeth-

erness of a stay-at-home movie night," Starfire said cheerfully. "I have brought you popcorn and non-cotton candy. Tell me, what sort of movie should we view?"

"Action!" Robin said.

"Comedy!" said Beast Boy.

"Sci-fi," Cyborg chimed in.

"Horror," said Raven.

Starfire smiled nervously. This wasn't going as smoothly as she had hoped. "Perhaps a double feature?"

Then Blackfire swept into the room.

"Forget the flicks, kids," she said. "We're going out!"

Blackfire walked right past Starfire — wearing purple shorts and a purple shirt, just like Starfire's!

"We are going out?" Starfire asked, confused. "Where did you — are those mine?"

Blackfire ignored her. "Heard about a party downtown," she told the other Titans. "Cool crowd. Hot music."

"Yeah!" cried Beast Boy.

"Why not?" Robin said.

"I'm in," said Cyborg.

Only Raven didn't reply.

"And it's in a creepy, run-down warehouse," Blackfire added.

Raven looked up from her book and raised her eyebrows. That was about as excited as Raven ever got about anything.

Beast Boy jumped up from the couch. "I am a party animal!" he cried, transforming into a gorilla to prove his point. The others got off the couch and followed Beast Boy to the elevator.

Starfire dropped her armload of snacks and DVDs. What was the use? She might as well go along with the others. Blackfire sidled up to her.

"Hey, sweetie," she said. "Raided your closet. Hope you don't mind me borrowing your look."

"Why not?" Starfire muttered. "You've already borrowed my friends."

When they arrived at the warehouse, the party

was in full swing. Dancing bodies filled the room. Flashing lights blinked on and off, and pounding music filled the air. Rows of windows lined the ceiling, so the night sky was clearly visible over- head.

"Step aside, earthlings," Blackfire called out. "The queen of the galaxy has arrived!"

Blackfire gracefully swept into the crowd and began to dance. The Titans followed her. Starfire found she couldn't get far without bumping into one of the dancers.

"Excuse me," she said. Then she felt a sharp pain in her foot. A boy pushed past her and kept walking. "Ow! You really should apologize after stepping on someone's foot."

Blackfire motioned to the Titans, who stood on the sidelines. "Now don't tell me you big-shot super heroes are afraid of a little dancing."

The boys took Blackfire's words as a challenge. Robin, Beast Boy, and Cyborg stepped onto the dance floor and began to groove. Only

Raven and Starfire stayed where they were.

"This party is pointless," Raven said.

Starfire was grateful to hear that. At least she'd have a friend to talk to while the boys were busy with her sister.

But just then, a pale boy wearing a black T-shirt with a ghost on it walked up to Raven.

"Everything is pointless," he said. "Want to go talk about it?"

Raven nodded, and she and the boy walked off. Starfire sighed and watched the dancers.

A boy in a green sweatshirt danced up to her.

"Hey, hot alien girl," he said. "You digging the scene?"

"I did not know we were supposed to bring shovels," Starfire replied.

The boy burst out laughing. Soon, everyone around them was laughing.

Starfire's face flushed red. She must have said something embarassing. She was always doing that. Earth language was so difficult to understand sometimes.

Suddenly, Starfire had to get away. Without another word, she ran outside.

Chapter Six

Not Wonderful

Looking at the sky always made Starfire feel better when she was sad. Somewhere out there was her home planet, Tamaran — a place where she had always managed to fit in. Starfire flew up to the roof of the warehouse and sat on the edge, gazing up at the stars.

"Perhaps I do not belong here after all," she said sadly.

A door swung open behind her and Robin stepped out. "Of course you don't. You belong down there having fun with the rest of us. What's wrong?" He walked over to Starfire and sat down next to her.

Starfire forced a smile. She didn't want Robin

to worry about her. "Nothing is wrong. Everything is wonderful. The pounding music and blinding lights are quite enjoyable." Then Starfire looked down at her boots. She couldn't lie to Robin. "Everything is *not* wonderful," Starfire said. "I am happy to see her, but Blackfire rules the video games, and she is able to share very depressing poems, and she knows the cool moves, and she always knows when people are not talking about shovels. And I am nothing like her!"

"No, you're not," Robin said kindly. He put a hand on Starfire's shoulder. "And I think —"

Just then, one of the windows on the roof opened up, and Blackfire flew through it. She wore a long pink wig over her dark hair.

"How do I look?" she asked.

"Pink," Robin said, annoyed. "Look, can you give us a minute here?"

The strains of a new tune came through the open window, and Blackfire squealed with delight. "Ooh, I love this song!" She flew over to Robin, grabbed him by the arm, and flew away with him before he could protest.

Starfire sighed and rested her chin in her hands. Talking with Robin always made her feel better. And now Blackfire had robbed her of that. It just wasn't fair!

Suddenly, Starfire heard a whooshing sound. She looked up — another pod was speeding toward her!

Chapter Seven

Pod Attack!

Back in the warehouse, Beast Boy was dancing to the beat. But something — animal instinct, probably — made him look up.

Through the window, he could see two shadows. One was Starfire. The other was another one of those pods. Its tentacles lashed out, wrapping around Starfire's waist. In a flash, it zoomed off with Starfire in its clutches.

Beast Boy turned to Cyborg. "Cy! Starfire is in trouble!"

Before either boy could react, a pod emerged from the depths of the warehouse. It quickly grabbed Beast Boy in its tentacles and flew off.

Cyborg chased after them. But a third pod side-

swiped Cyborg, sending him smashing into a wall.

The pod that held Beast Boy zoomed past Raven, who was leaning against some wooden crates and talking to the boy in the ghost shirt. At the sight of the pod, the boy ran off. But Raven sprang into action. She floated up in the air, and used her powers to levitate the two crates. Then she sent them hurtling toward the pod.

Raven had perfect aim. The crates slammed into the metal capsule, jarring the pod and freeing Beast Boy, who tumbled to the cement floor.

But the fight was just beginning. With a sickening crash, the pod holding Starfire broke through the glass window. Both the pod and Star landed inside a large wooden crate. At the same time, Cyborg attacked another pod with a powerful robot punch.

In the next instant, Starfire flew out of the crate. The pod rose up beneath her. She blasted it with powerful jolts of green energy from her hands. The pod flew backward, nearly knocking

into Beast Boy. But the agile Titan jumped out of
the way. When he landed, he had transformed into

a muscular green tiger. The tiger lunged at the pod, swiping at its metal body with his sharp claws.

But the pod escaped. It swooped around Cyborg and hovered in the air next to the other two pods. Then all three pods surrounded Starfire.

Starfire wasn't going to give up. She soared underneath the pods, but they lined up and flew after her.

Cyborg stopped them by grabbing on to the tentacles of all three pods, stopping them in midair. He quickly hurled one of the pods out of the way. With lightning speed, he tossed a second pod aside, but the third pod was ready for Cyborg. It spun like a top in the air, then slammed into him with incredible force. The largest Titan went crashing through a concrete wall.

Being partially made of steel had its advantages, and Cyborg got through the collision with just a few scratches. He found himself in a stairwell — with Robin and Blackfire.

"What's going on?" Robin asked.

"Remember that thing that attacked Star? It had friends," Cyborg said, clambering to his feet. He ran back through the hole in the wall.

Robin started to follow — and noticed that Blackfire was still at the top of the stairs, not moving.

"Didn't you hear him?" Robin asked. "Your sister needs help."

"Oh, right," Blackfire said. She tore off the pink wig and flew after Robin and Cyborg.

Back in the warehouse, one of the pods had grabbed Starfire again. The pod crashed through the windows on the ceiling. The jolt sent Starfire tumbling from the tentacles. She landed inside a metal Dumpster on the roof, and the lid slammed shut above her.

The pod grabbed the Dumpster in its tentacles and flew toward the other two pods. The three pods made a move to fly off — but a red boomerang stopped them. The boomerang sliced through two of the tentacles on the first pod,

sending the Dumpster slamming down onto the roof. Then the boomerang sailed back into the hands of the person who threw it — Robin.

Robin, Cyborg, Beast Boy, and Raven faced the pods, ready to fight. But Blackfire flew right over them, aiming straight at the pods.

BLAST! BLAST! BLAST!

Violet light shot from Blackfire's eyes. Each blast made contact with a pod. One by one, the pods exploded into pieces. Shards of smoking wreckage littered the roof.

The Teen Titans ran up to Blackfire.

"Oh, yeah!" Cyborg cheered. "Good times!"

"Nice shooting, Tex," Beast Boy said admiringly.

"How did you know where to hit them?" Robin asked.

Blackfire shrugged. "Lucky guess."

"We could use luck like that," Cyborg said. "Maybe you should join the team."

"Me?" Blackfire said, her voice full of surprise. "A Teen Titan?"

Starfire's head popped out of the Dumpster. Had she heard right? Her sister, a Teen Titan? Maybe Blackfire was a better fighter than she after all.

"Blackfire will make a better Titan than I ever was," Starfire said sadly. She took off into the night sky — alone.

Chapter Eight

Captured!

Starfire flew to Teen Titans' headquarters. She filled a backpack with as many of her belongings as she could, then headed for the roof. She wasn't sure where she was going — she just knew the Teen Titans didn't need her anymore. Not with Blackfire around.

Suddenly, Starfire heard a voice behind her.

"Were you just going to leave without saying good-bye?"

It was Robin. Seeing him made Starfire suddenly feel silly for leaving. She didn't want to, really. She loved being a Teen Titan. But living in Blackfire's shadow was too hard. If only she could make Robin understand.

Starfire floated down to the roof and let her backpack fall. "Robin, I —" she began. Then her words turned to a scream of terror.

A long, low spaceship emerged from the clouds. A tall, red alien stood on top of the ship as it coasted toward them. Starfire didn't know who he was but she sensed that he was trouble. A long, green tentacle shot out of the alien's claw and wrapped around Starfire before she could move out of the way. She tried to blast it but the tentacle covered her eyes, making it impossible to attack. Then the tentacle began to pull Starfire up toward the ship.

Robin couldn't fly, but he ran across the roof and jumped as high as he could, hoping to grab Starfire's leg. He missed, but managed to attach himself to the underside of the ship.

Up on top of the ship, the alien put Starfire inside a glass dome. Nearby, another alien sat beneath a glass window, piloting the ship.

The pilot talked into a microphone. "Prepare to leave the Earth's orbit. We have the Tamaranian girl."

The other alien looked through the glass at Starfire. "Once we have returned to Centauri, you'll pay for what you have done."

At that moment, Robin climbed up on top of the ship.

"Nobody is taking my friend away," Robin growled.

The alien swiped at Robin with his huge claw. Robin jumped over the alien's head and landed on the other side of him, near Starfire. The alien responded by blasting Robin with fiery lasers shot

from his claws. Robin dodged to the left and right, avoiding the attack.

The angry alien charged at Robin. The alien might be big and powerful, but small and agile as he was, Robin had the advantage. He dodged out of the way again, and the alien slammed his claw into the glass dome instead of Robin. Robin used the opportunity to deliver a martial-arts punch to the alien's arm. Sparks shot from the metal arm, but the punch didn't do much damage.

The alien attacked Robin again, this time shooting a green tentacle from its claw. Once again, Robin dodged out of the way.

This time, the tentacle made contact with a power cell protruding from the top of the ship. There was a sizzling sound as the cell short-circuited. The ship began to wobble in the air.

"I cannot control it!" the pilot cried.

The ship began to sink lower and lower. The pilot steered toward an open field, but it was clear the ship was about to crash.

Robin acted quickly. He pressed a red button on the metal dome holding Starfire. When the dome opened up, Robin pulled off the tentacle that held Starfire. Then he pulled her out.

"Come on!" Robin cried.

Starfire nodded. She grabbed Robin's arm and they flew off the alien ship.

Seconds later, the ship crashed into the dirt!

Chapter Nine

The Wrong Girl

Robin and Starfire landed on the ground near the smoking spaceship.

"Star! Robin!" Beast Boy cried.

They turned to see Beast Boy, Cyborg, and Raven approaching.

"You guys okay?" Cyborg asked.

Before they could answer, the two aliens stepped out of the wrecked ship and walked toward them.

"Titans, get ready!" Robin cried, striking a battle pose.

One of the aliens spoke up. "In the name of the Centauri empire, you are all under arrest!"

The Titans looked at one another, confused. Under arrest?

"Uh . . . you guys can't be the good guys," said Beast Boy. "We're the good guys."

"And we are Centauri police," said the alien.

The second alien pointed to Starfire. "The Tamaranian girl is a liar and a thief. She has committed high crimes throughout the entire Centauri system."

"I have never even been to the Centauri moons!" Starfire protested.

Robin took the green diamond from around Starfire's neck. He dangled it in front of her face.

"But I know someone who has," he said.

Starfire gasped. Blackfire had gotten the diamond from the Centauri moons — she had told Starfire herself!

Robin turned to the aliens. "You've been chasing the wrong girl. Where's Blackfire?"

Beast Boy pointed to the sky, where a slender figure was flying into the distance. "Uhh . . . "

"Don't worry, Star," Robin said. "She won't get away with this."

"No, she will not," Starfire said firmly. Then she sped off after her sister.

Blackfire was fast, but Starfire was faster. She flew in front of her sister, blocking her path.

"Hello, Sister," Starfire said, her green eyes blazing.

"Ah, you're mad," Blackfire said. "I know I should have told you I was leaving, but you know how I hate good-byes, and —"

"You are a criminal and you were going to let me take your place in jail!" Starfire said angrily.

Blackfire shrugged. "Oh. Well, yeah."

"You will give back what you have stolen and turn yourself in to the police," Starfire said.

"And what will you do if I don't?" Blackfire asked. But before Starfire could answer, Blackfire shot a violet blast from her eyes, hitting her sister

in the chest.

Starfire tumbled backward, but she quickly recovered and faced Blackfire.

"I always was the better fighter," Blackfire said.

"Not anymore!" Starfire cried.

BLAST! BLAST! BLAST! Starfire attacked her sister with shot after shot of green laser light from her eyes. She made sure to hit Blackfire's hands each time so that her sister couldn't power up and fight back.

Blackfire looked stunned. Starfire's attack was relentless. Her eyes glowed violet as she prepared to defend herself — but she didn't have a chance to. A green tentacle appeared out of nowhere and wrapped around Blackfire's waist. Blackfire cried out in alarm.

The aliens had regained control of their ship. The alien holding Blackfire dragged her aboard.

"Farewell, Sister," Starfire called out. "Although you did betray and attack me, it was still very nice to see you."

Blackfire's eyes blazed with burning violet light. "Next time it won't be so nice!" she shouted angrily. "I *will* get out of jail, little sister, and I *will* get even!"

Then she disappeared inside the Centauri ship.

Chapter Ten

A Place for Starfire

Back at headquarters, the rest of the Titans went to sleep, but Starfire sat on the roof, looking at the sky.

Blackfire was out there somewhere, in big trouble. So many things had happened in the last few days. It was hard to believe it had all been real.

Before she knew it, the sun began to rise over the river.

It's so beautiful, Starfire thought.

"Hey, how are you doing?" Robin asked, coming up behind her.

"I am sad for my sister," Starfire said.

"And for yourself?" Robin asked.

Starfire sighed. "I am just glad that the truth

was discovered before I was replaced."

"What are you talking about?" Robin asked, coming up behind her.

Starfire turned to her friend. "Well, you — everyone was having such fun with her, and then Cyborg said —"

Robin stopped her. "Look, your sister was . . . interesting. But she could never take your place. No one could ever take your place."

Robin smiled and Starfire smiled back. For the first time, she felt like she belonged here — really belonged.

The two friends turned back to the rising sun. Starfire felt happy to be here on Earth to greet a new day — and happy to be a member of the Teen Titans.